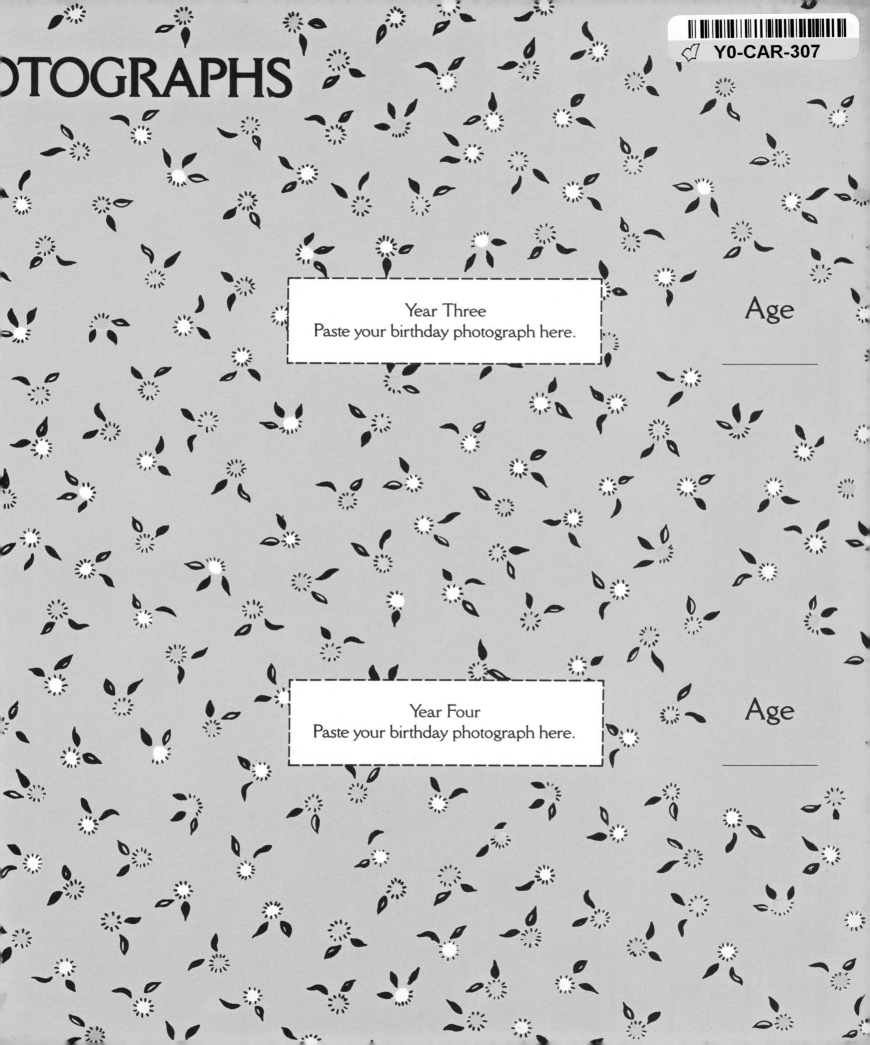

PHOTOGRAPHS

Y0-CAR-307

Year Three
Paste your birthday photograph here.

Age
_____

Year Four
Paste your birthday photograph here.

Age
_____

Copyright © 1988 by The Metropolitan Museum of Art
Text copyright © 1988 by Dian G. Smith

All rights reserved. No part of this book may be
reproduced or transmitted in any form or by any
means, electronic or mechanical, including
photocopying, recording, or by any information
storage and retrieval system, without permission in
writing from the Publishers.

Published by The Metropolitan Museum of Art and
Charles Scribner's Sons, Macmillan Publishing
Company, 866 Third Avenue, New York, NY 10022
Collier Macmillan Canada, Inc.

3   5   7   9   11   13   15   17   19   20   18   16   14   12   10   8   6   4

ISBN 0-684-19046-X (Scribners)
ISBN 0-87099-527-8 (MMA)

Produced by the Department of Special Publications,
The Metropolitan Museum of Art
Typeset by Nassau Typographers, New York
Printed and bound by A. Mondadori, Verona, Italy

The drawings in this book are adapted from illustrations
by Marie Madeleine Franc-Nohain for a baby book
published in Paris in 1914. The book, *Le Journal de
Bébé,* is in the collections of The Metropolitan Museum
of Art.

The Elisha Whittelsey Collection, The Elisha Whittelsey
Fund, 1977 (1977.588.1)

MMA 11-01321-6

# HAPPY BIRTHDAY TO ME!

## A Four-Year Record Book
## for Birthday Boys and Girls

by Dian G. Smith
Designed by Douglas Sardo

THE METROPOLITAN MUSEUM OF ART
CHARLES SCRIBNER'S SONS
NEW YORK

# THE BIRTHDAY ☐ BOY ☐ GIRL

My name is _____

My parents picked it because _____

_____

My parents almost called me _____

My friends call me _____

Here are some silly names people call me: _____

_____

I was born in _____
city          state

on _____
    month     day     year

on a _____ at _____ ☐ A.M.
day of the week     time    ☐ P.M.

This is how it looks
on the clock.

(Draw in the hands.)

# This is a picture of me as a tiny baby.

## Some other people who were born on my birthday are

_____    _____

_____    _____

_____    _____

_____    _____

_____

If you don't know anyone who shares your birthday, look for the *Biography Almanac* in your library. It lists the birthdays of more than 24,000 famous people.

My great-grandfather

My great-grandmother

My great-grandfather

My great-grandmother

My grandfather

My grandmother

My father

# Here is my family tree.

Write in your name and the names of your parents, grandparents, and great-grandparents. If you are named after any of these relatives, mark their names with a star.

My great-grandfather

My great-grandmother

My great-grandfather

My great-grandmother

My grandfather

My grandmother

My mother

# MY BIRTHDAY

——— ——— ——— ———
Year

Today I am ———— years old.

This year my birthday is on a
☐ Monday   ☐ Tuesday   ☐ Wednesday
☐ Thursday   ☐ Friday   ☐ Saturday   ☐ Sunday

This year, at the exact moment of my birth, I was

☐ tying my shoe   ☐ planting string beans   ☐ sleeping

☐ frying an egg   ☐ bouncing   ☐ ————————————
something else

(Draw today's weather.)

Outside
☐ the sun is shining
☐ the wind is blowing
☐ rain is falling
☐ snow is falling
☐ french fries are dancing
☐ ————————————
something else

# Here are my favorites this year.

My best friend: _____

My favorite babysitter: _____

My favorite food: _____

My favorite game: _____

My favorite bug: _____

My favorite animal: _____

My favorite _____
something else

This is what is
happening in
the world today.

(Paste in a
front-page headline
from today's
newspaper.)

The best thing that happened to

me this year was _____

_____

The worst thing that happened to

me this year was _____

_____

The best thing I learned how to do

this year is _____

_____

# GETTING BIGG

I am _____ feet and _____ inches tall.

My shoes are size

| | | | |
|---|---|---|---|
| 4 | 8 | 1 | 36 |
| 10 | 13 | 3 | 9 |
| 73 | 12 | 2 | 6 |
| 5 | 97 | 7 | 11 |

(Circle one.)

My clothes are size

| | | | |
|---|---|---|---|
| 12 | 3 | 5 | 82 |
| 2 | 23 | 6 | 10 |
| 9 | 7 | 14 | 1 |
| 11 | 4 | 8 | 45 |

(Circle one.)

I now have    0    1    2    3    25    100    a zillion    freckles.

(Circle one.)

I am taller than    ☐ a fire hydrant

☐ my father

☐ a frog

☐ a cow

☐ a teddy bear

☐ _____
something else

# R ALL THE TIME

I weigh _____ pounds.

I am heavier than ☐ a grasshopper ☐ a telephone

☐ a tractor ☐ my mother

☐ a book

☐ _____
something else

I now have    0    5    10    15    20    100    teeth.
(Circle one.)

### SEE HOW YOU GROW

✸ Make a measuring wall to record your height. Ask a grown-up to help you mark feet and inches on a wall in your room or in a closet starting at the floor and going up to six feet. Stand against the wall on your birthday and have someone mark your height and record the date.

✸ Ask someone to take a picture of you standing in front of your measuring wall. Paste this birthday photograph inside the front cover of this book.

✸ Trace your hand in the space provided inside the back cover of this book.

At the end of four years you will see how much you have grown!

— 56 in.
— 55 in.
— 54 in.
— 53 in.
— 52 in.
— 51 in.
— 50 in.
— 49 in.
— 4 ft.
— 47 in.
— 46 in.
— 45 in.
— 43 in.
— 42 in.
— 41 in.
— 40 in.
— 39 in.
— 38 in.
— 37 in.
— 3 ft.
— 35 in.
— 34 in.
— 33 in.
— 32 in.
— 31 in.
— 30 in.
— 29 in.

# MY BIRTHDAY

This is how I celebrated my birthday:

☐ an outing          ☐ an adventure

☐ a party with friends

☐ a safari          ☐ a frog-jumping contest

☐ a sleep-over          ☐ _____

something else

I celebrated my birthday

on _____ at _____

date          time

Here is my invitation.

(Paste it in.)

These are the friends and relatives I invited:

_____  _____  _____

_____  _____  _____

_____  _____  _____

_____  _____  _____

This is where I celebrated my birthday: _____

_____

This is how it was decorated: _____

_____

## MAKE A BIRTHDAY COLLAGE

Collect scraps from your party decorations and wrapping paper. Make a colorful design by pasting them on a party plate or a piece of cardboard. Write the date at the bottom and hang up your collage to remind you of your birthday celebration.

Choose your favorite birthday card and write the date on its back. Put the card in the souvenir pocket inside the back cover of this book.

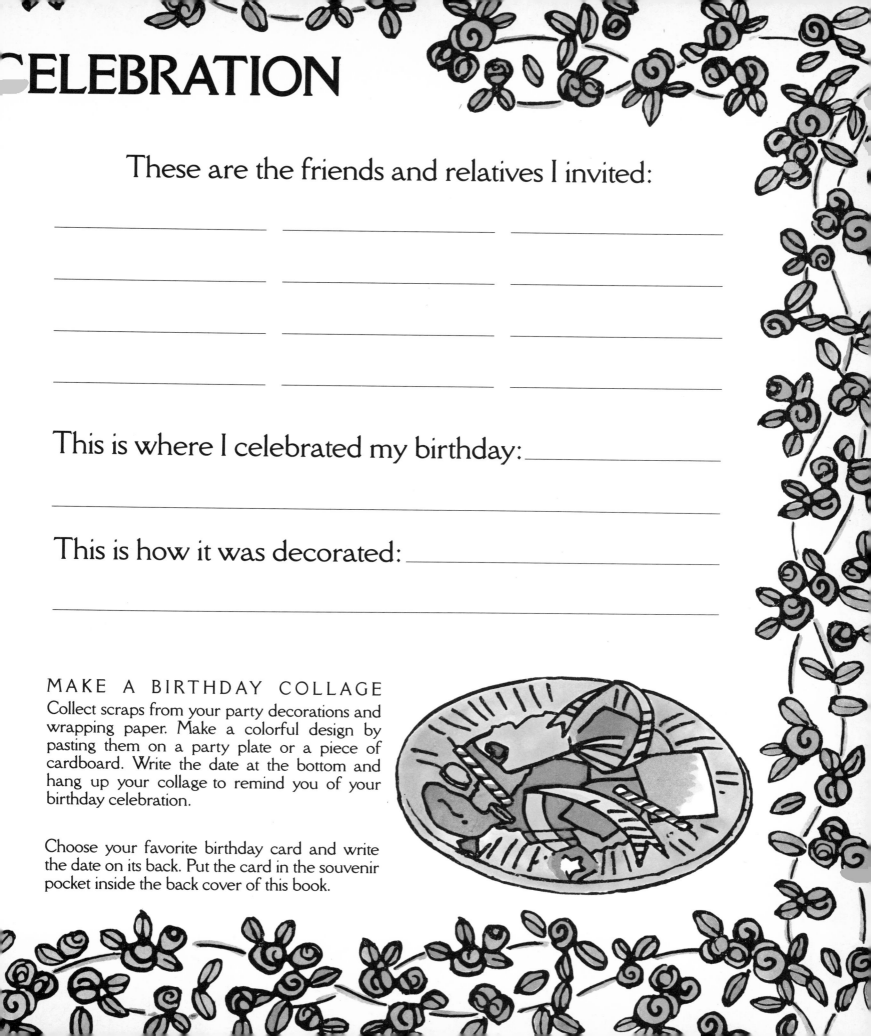

This is what we did at my birthday celebration:

_____

_____

_____

The best part was _____

_____

We ate
- ☐ sandwiches
- ☐ snails
- ☐ cake and ice cream
- ☐ pebbles
- ☐ _____ something else

My birthday cake was
- ☐ chocolate
- ☐ vanilla
- ☐ lemon
- ☐ spinach
- ☐ _____ something else

The frosting was
- ☐ chocolate
- ☐ vanilla
- ☐ strawberry
- ☐ toothpaste
- ☐ _____ something else

Here is a picture of my birthday cake.

I blew out _____ candles.
how many?

This was my wish. (Write it on a slip of paper or ask a grown-up to help you write it. Fold it and tape it in here.)

TOP SECRET

The wish I made last year ☐ came true
☐ sort of came true ☐ didn't come true
☐ Oops! I don't remember.

# Here is my favorite birthday picture.

Put extra pictures
in the pocket inside the
back cover of this book.

# These are the presents I received:

# The very best thing that happened today was

_____

# NEXT YEAR

Next year I will be _____ years old.
By my next birthday, I hope I will be able to

- [ ] stay up late
- [ ] yodel
- [ ] blow a bubble
- [ ] ice-skate
- [ ] run faster than this year
- [ ] do a somersault
- [ ] build an igloo
- [ ] pilot a spaceship
- [ ] ride a giraffe
- [ ] skip backward
- [ ] capture a rhinoceros
- [ ] bake a cake
- [ ] count to a zillion
- [ ] spin a top
- [ ] _____ something else
- [ ] float on a cloud

# MY BIRTHDAY

———— ———— ———— ————
Year

Today I am ———— years old.

This year my birthday is on a

☐ Monday  ☐ Tuesday  ☐ Wednesday

☐ Thursday  ☐ Friday  ☐ Saturday  ☐ Sunday

Outside  ☐ rain is falling  ☐ the sun is shining

☐ snow is falling  ☐ the wind is blowing

☐ bananas are flying

☐ ————————————
something else

This year, at the exact moment of my birth, I was

☐ sleeping  ☐ making mud pies

☐ burying a treasure  ☐ singing

☐ petting a dinosaur

☐ ————————————
something else

# Here are my favorites this year.

My best friend: _____

My favorite babysitter: _____

My favorite food: _____

My favorite color: _____

My favorite song: _____

My favorite mischief: _____

_____

The best thing that happened to me this year was _____

_____

The worst thing that happened to me this year was _____

_____

The best thing I learned how to do this year is _____

_____

## This is what is happening in the world today.

(Paste in a front-page headline from today's newspaper.)

# GETTING BIGG

I am _____ feet and _____ inches tall.

I am _____ inches ☐ taller / ☐ shorter than last year.

I am taller than

☐ a milk carton     ☐ my mother     ☐ a toothbrush

☐ a duck     ☐ a brontosaurus     ☐ _____
something else

My shoes are size

_____

My clothes are size

_____

# ALL THE TIME

I weigh _____ pounds.

I weigh _____ pounds ☐ more ☐ less than last year.

This is a picture of my smile.

Draw a picture of your smile showing how many teeth you have. Color your permanent teeth red.

I am heavier than

☐ a crab

☐ a cough drop

☐ a lawn mower   ☐ my father

☐ a pocketbook

☐ _____ something else

This is how many baby teeth fell out this year:

_____

This is how many new teeth grew in this year:

_____

REMEMBER!

☼ Mark your height on your measuring wall and write the year beside it.

☼ Ask someone to take a picture of you standing in front of your measuring wall. Paste this birthday photograph inside the front cover of this book.

☼ Trace your hand in the space provided inside the back cover of this book.

How much have you grown?

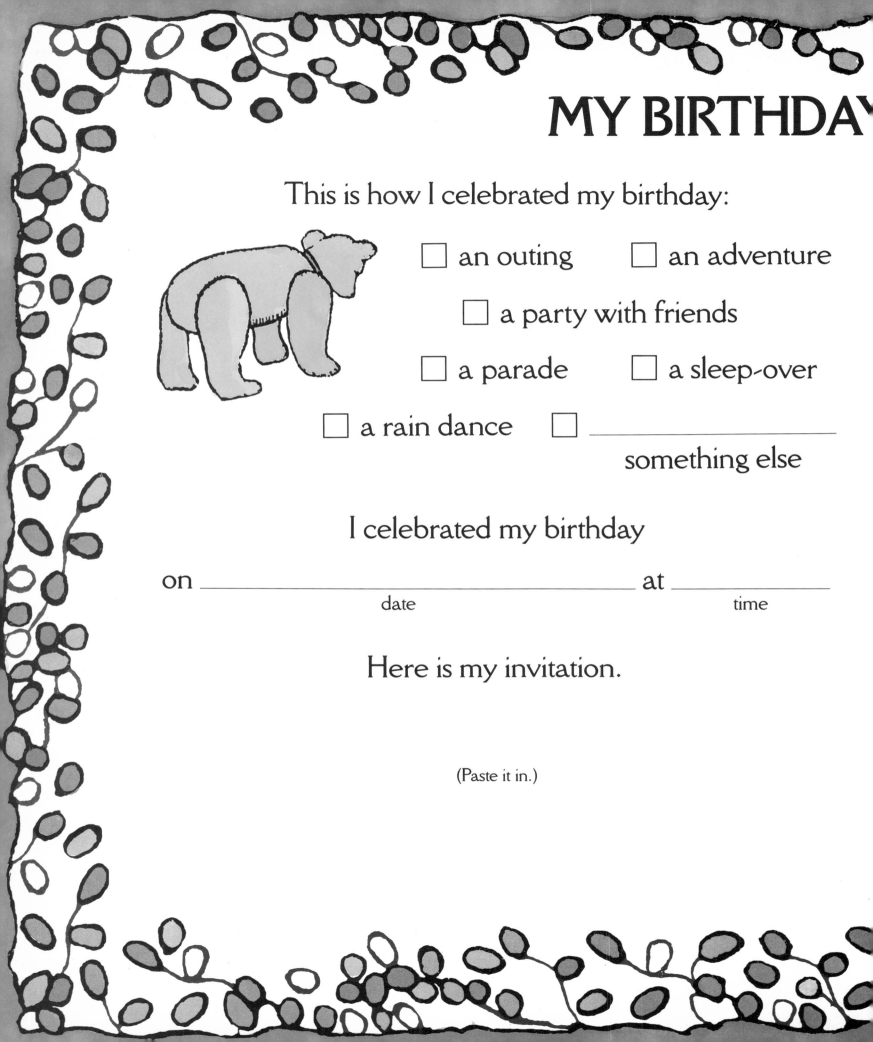

# MY BIRTHDAY

This is how I celebrated my birthday:

☐ an outing    ☐ an adventure

☐ a party with friends

☐ a parade    ☐ a sleep-over

☐ a rain dance    ☐ _____

something else

I celebrated my birthday

on _____ at _____

date                                              time

Here is my invitation.

(Paste it in.)

# CELEBRATION

These are the friends and relatives I invited:

_____    _____    _____

_____    _____    _____

_____    _____    _____

_____    _____    _____

This is where I celebrated my birthday:_____

_____

This is how it was decorated:_____

_____

## MAKE A BIRTHDAY CARD BANNER

Put your birthday cards in a straight line on the floor. Cut a piece of ribbon that stretches from the first card to the last one, with an extra six inches of ribbon at each end. Tape the cards to the ribbon, then hang your banner on a wall or over a doorway.

Choose your favorite birthday card and write the date on its back. Put the card in the souvenir pocket inside the back cover of this book.

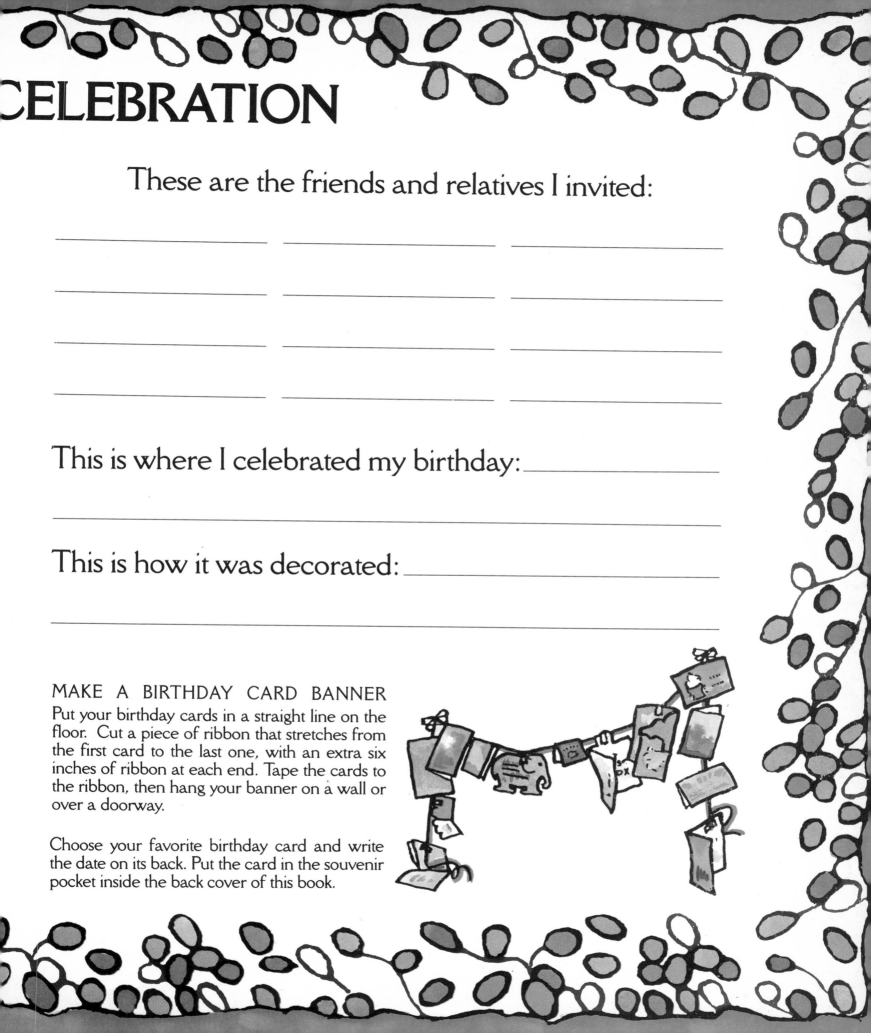

This is what we did at my birthday celebration:

_____

_____

_____

The best part was _____

_____

We ate
- ☐ shoelaces
- ☐ sandwiches
- ☐ cake and ice cream
- ☐ bumblebees
- ☐ _____ something else

My birthday cake was
- ☐ chocolate
- ☐ vanilla
- ☐ strawberry
- ☐ pickle
- ☐ _____ something else

The frosting was
- ☐ chocolate
- ☐ vanilla
- ☐ strawberry
- ☐ mud
- ☐ _____ something else

Here is a picture of my birthday cake.

I blew out _____ candles.
how many?

This was my wish.

(Write it on a slip of paper or ask
a grown-up to help you write it.
Fold it and tape it in here.)

TOP SECRET

The wish I made last year

☐ came true
☐ didn't come true
☐ sort of came true

# Here is my favorite birthday picture.

Put extra pictures
in the pocket inside the
back cover of this book.

## These are the presents I received:

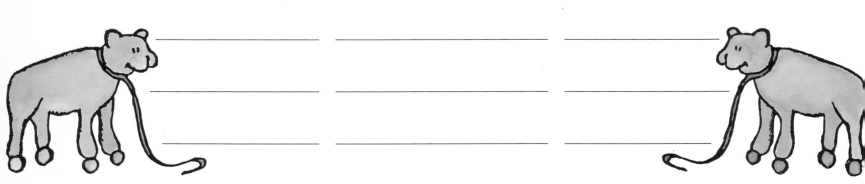

_____ _____ _____

_____ _____ _____

_____ _____ _____

## The very best thing that happened today was

_____

# NEXT YEAR

Next year I will be _____ years old.
By my next birthday, I hope I will be able to

- ☐ do jumping jacks
- ☐ stand on my head
- ☐ fly
- ☐ read a book
- ☐ star on TV
- ☐ finish a big puzzle
- ☐ get an allowance
- ☐ sleep in a tent
- ☐ jump farther
- ☐ go to college
- ☐ drive a bulldozer
- ☐ capture pirates
- ☐ become invisible
- ☐ snap my fingers
- ☐ _____ something else

# MY BIRTHDAY

_____ _____ _____
Year

Today I am _____ years old.

This year my birthday is on a

☐ Monday ☐ Tuesday ☐ Wednesday

☐ Thursday ☐ Friday ☐ Saturday ☐ Sunday

Outside ☐ the sun is shining ☐ rain is falling

☐ the wind is blowing ☐ snow is falling

☐ trees are disappearing ☐ _____
something else

This year, at the exact moment of my birth, I was

☐ playing a kettledrum ☐ taming a lion

☐ sleeping ☐ scratching a ☐ counting jellybeans
mosquito bite

☐ _____
something else

# Here are my favorites this year.

My best friend: _____

My favorite babysitter: _____

My favorite teacher: _____

My favorite dinosaur: _____

My favorite book: _____

My favorite clothes: _____

_____

This is what is happening in the world today.

(Paste in a front-page headline from today's newspaper.)

The best thing that happened to me this year was _____

_____

The worst thing that happened to me this year was _____

_____

The best thing I learned how to do this year is _____

_____

# GETTING BIGG

I am _____ feet and _____ inches tall.

I am _____ inches taller than last year.

My shoes are size

| | | | |
|---|---|---|---|
| 62 | 5 | 12 | 3 |
| 10 | 2 | 93 | 11 |
| 8 | 86 | 4 | 7 |
| 13 | 1 | 9 | 6 |

(Circle one.)

My clothes are size

| | | | |
|---|---|---|---|
| 9 | 6 | 58 | 14 |
| 1 | 26 | 7 | 5 |
| 75 | 3 | 12 | 8 |
| 4 | 11 | 2 | 10 |

(Circle one.)

I am taller than a

☐ door

☐ canary

☐ fishing pole

☐ tulip

☐ candle

☐ _____
something else

# ALL THE TIME

I weigh _____ pounds.

I weigh _____ pounds more than last year.

I am heavier than a ☐ lobster

☐ baboon          ☐ lamp

☐ cupcake          ☐ kangaroo

☐ _____
something else

I now have   0   1   2   3   25   100   a zillion   freckles.
(Circle one.)

Draw a picture of your
face that shows all of your
freckles.

### REMEMBER!

☼ Mark your height on your measuring wall and write the year beside it.

☼ Ask someone to take a picture of you standing in front of your measuring wall. Paste this birthday photograph inside the front cover of this book.

☼ Trace your hand in the space provided inside the back cover of this book.

How much have you grown?

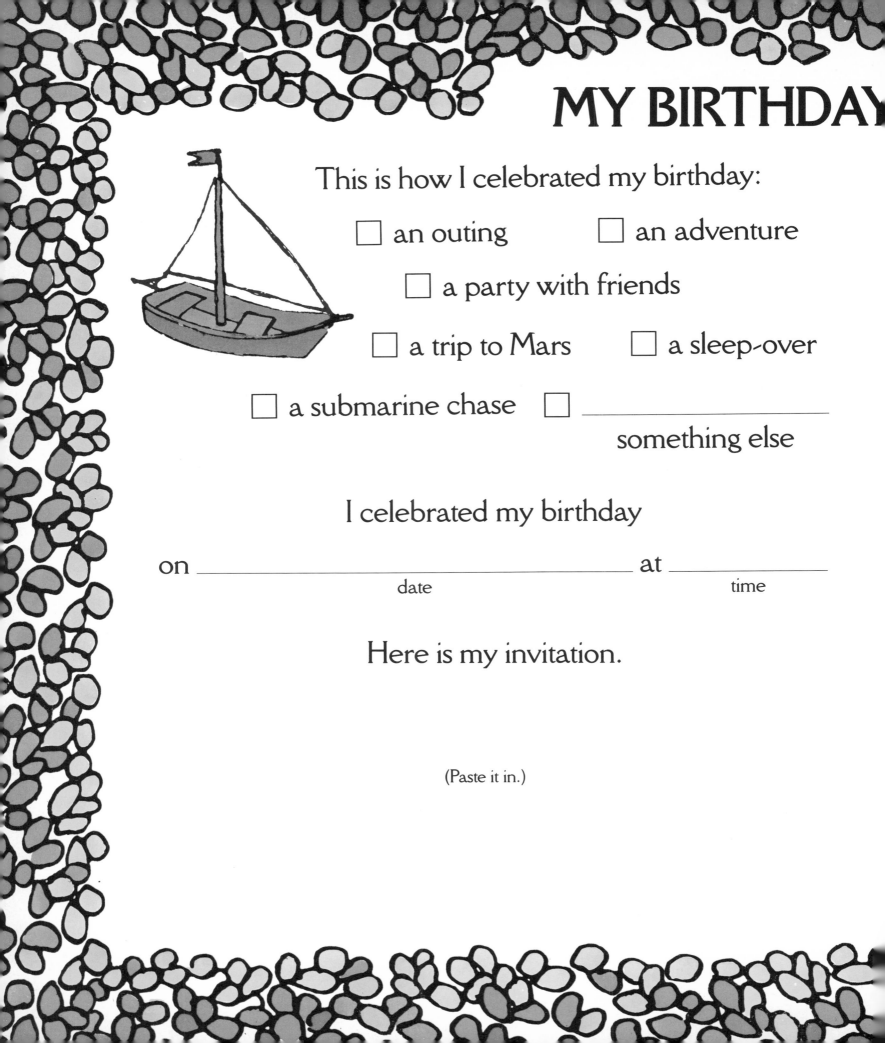

This is how I celebrated my birthday:

☐ an outing        ☐ an adventure

☐ a party with friends

☐ a trip to Mars        ☐ a sleep-over

☐ a submarine chase        ☐ _____

something else

I celebrated my birthday

on _____ at _____

date        time

Here is my invitation.

(Paste it in.)

# CELEBRATION

These are the friends and relatives I invited:

_____   _____   _____

_____   _____   _____

_____   _____   _____

_____

This is where I celebrated my birthday: _____

_____

This is how it was decorated: _____

_____

### BIRTHDAY AUTOGRAPHS

Write your birth date on an old white sheet and use this as a tablecloth. Ask your friends to decorate it when they first come in by signing their names and drawing pictures or designs or writing notes. Use laundry pens or other permanent markers. Protect the table by placing a plastic cloth or several layers of newspaper beneath the sheet.

Choose your favorite birthday card and write the date on its back. Put the card in the souvenir pocket inside the back cover of this book.

This is what we did at my birthday celebration:

_____

_____

_____

The best part was _____

_____

We ate
- ☐ sandwiches
- ☐ leaves
- ☐ cake and ice cream
- ☐ lizards
- ☐ _____
  something else

My birthday cake was
- ☐ chocolate
- ☐ vanilla
- ☐ spice
- ☐ licorice
- ☐ _____
  something else

The frosting was
- ☐ chocolate
- ☐ vanilla
- ☐ strawberry
- ☐ ketchup
- ☐ _____
  something else

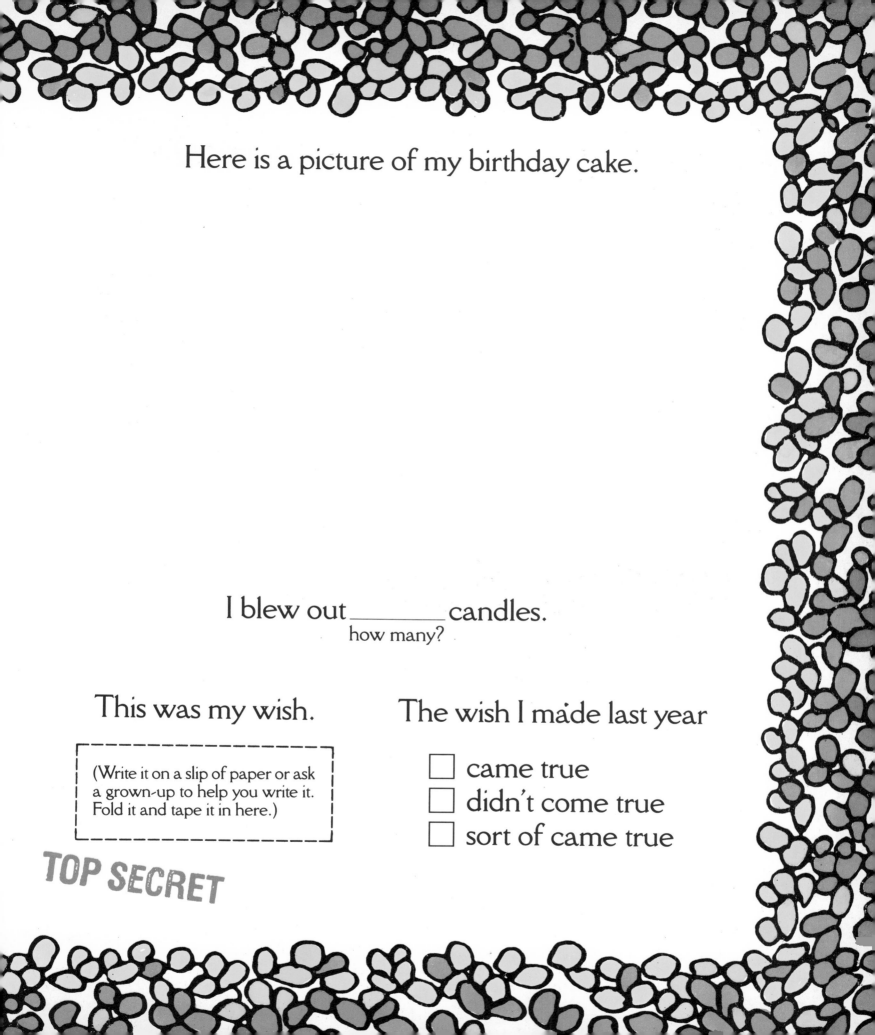

Here is a picture of my birthday cake.

I blew out _____ candles.
how many?

This was my wish.

(Write it on a slip of paper or ask a grown-up to help you write it. Fold it and tape it in here.)

TOP SECRET

The wish I made last year

☐ came true
☐ didn't come true
☐ sort of came true

# Here is my favorite birthday picture.

Put extra pictures
in the pocket inside the
back cover of this book.

## These are the presents I received:

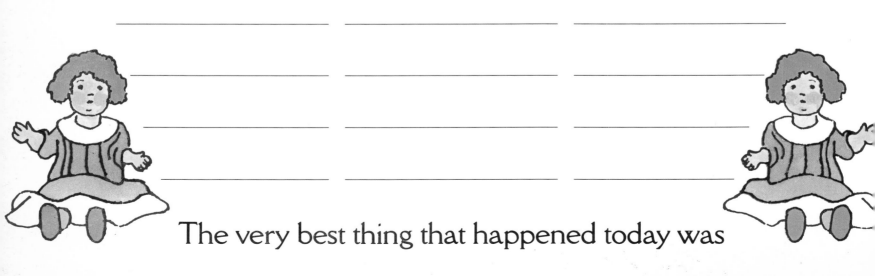

_____  _____  _____

_____  _____  _____

_____  _____  _____

_____  _____  _____

## The very best thing that happened today was

_____

# NEXT YEAR

Next year I will be _____ years old.
By my next birthday, I hope I will be able to

☐ ride a porpoise

☐ meet an alien    ☐ ski

☐ wiggle my ears

☐ play the piano

☐ whistle "Happy Birthday"

☐ hit a home run

☐ go around the world

☐ conduct an orchestra

☐ swim underwater

☐ do a cartwheel    ☐ train a seal

☐ _____
something else

☐ ride a surfboard

☐ write a book

# MY BIRTHDAY

_____ _____ _____ _____
Year

Today I am _____ years old.

This year my birthday is on a

☐ Monday  ☐ Tuesday  ☐ Wednesday

☐ Thursday  ☐ Friday  ☐ Saturday  ☐ Sunday

Outside  ☐ the sun is shining  ☐ the wind is blowing

☐ rain is falling  ☐ lampposts are melting

☐ snow is falling  ☐ _____
something else

This year, at the exact moment of my birth, I was

☐ climbing a mountain

☐ taking a bath

☐ sleeping

☐ hugging a puppy

☐ kissing a tadpole

☐ _____
something else

# Here are my favorites this year.

My best friend: _____

My favorite babysitter: _____

My favorite teacher: _____

My favorite joke: _____

My favorite movie: _____

My favorite food: _____

_____

## This is what is happening in the world today.

```
(Paste in a front-page headline from today's newspaper.)
```

The best thing that happened to me this year was _____

_____

The worst thing that happened to me this year was _____

_____

The best thing I learned how to do this year is _____

_____

# GETTING BIGG

I am _____ feet and _____ inches tall.

I am _____ inches taller than last year.

This is a picture of my smile.

I am taller than a

☐ rabbit      ☐ tree

☐ spoon      ☐ scarecrow

☐ fish      ☐ _____
                something else

Draw a picture of your
smile showing how many
teeth you have. Color your
permanent teeth red.

This is how many
baby teeth fell out this year:

_____

This is how many
new teeth grew in this year:

_____

### REMEMBER!

❋ Mark your height on your measuring wall
and write the year beside it.

❋ Ask someone to take a picture of you
standing in front of your measuring wall.
Paste this birthday photograph inside the
front cover of this book.

❋ Trace your hand in the space provided
inside the back cover of this book.

How much have you grown?

# ALL THE TIME

I weigh _____ pounds.

I weigh _____ pounds more than last year.

I am heavier than a

☐ football          ☐ seashell

☐ doghouse          ☐ tyrannosaurus

☐ sponge            ☐ _____
                      something else

My shoes are size

_____

My clothes are size

_____

# MY BIRTHDAY

This is how I celebrated my birthday:

☐ an outing      ☐ an adventure

☐ a party with friends

☐ a spy mission      ☐ a sleep-over

☐ a ride on a crocodile    ☐ _____

something else

I celebrated my birthday

on _____ at _____
date                     time

Here is my invitation.

(Paste it in.)

# CELEBRATION

These are the friends and relatives I invited:

_____  _____  _____

_____  _____  _____

_____  _____  _____

_____  _____  _____

This is where I celebrated my birthday:_____

_____

This is how it was decorated: _____

_____

### MAKE A NEW BIRTHDAY RECORD BOOK FOR THE YEARS TO COME

Use a ring binder that will hold about 25 to 30 pieces of paper. Choose heavy paper, even if you have to punch the holes yourself. Copy what you liked in this book and add ideas of your own. Record many more happy birthdays!

Choose your favorite birthday card and write the date on its back. Put the card in the souvenir pocket inside the back cover of this book.

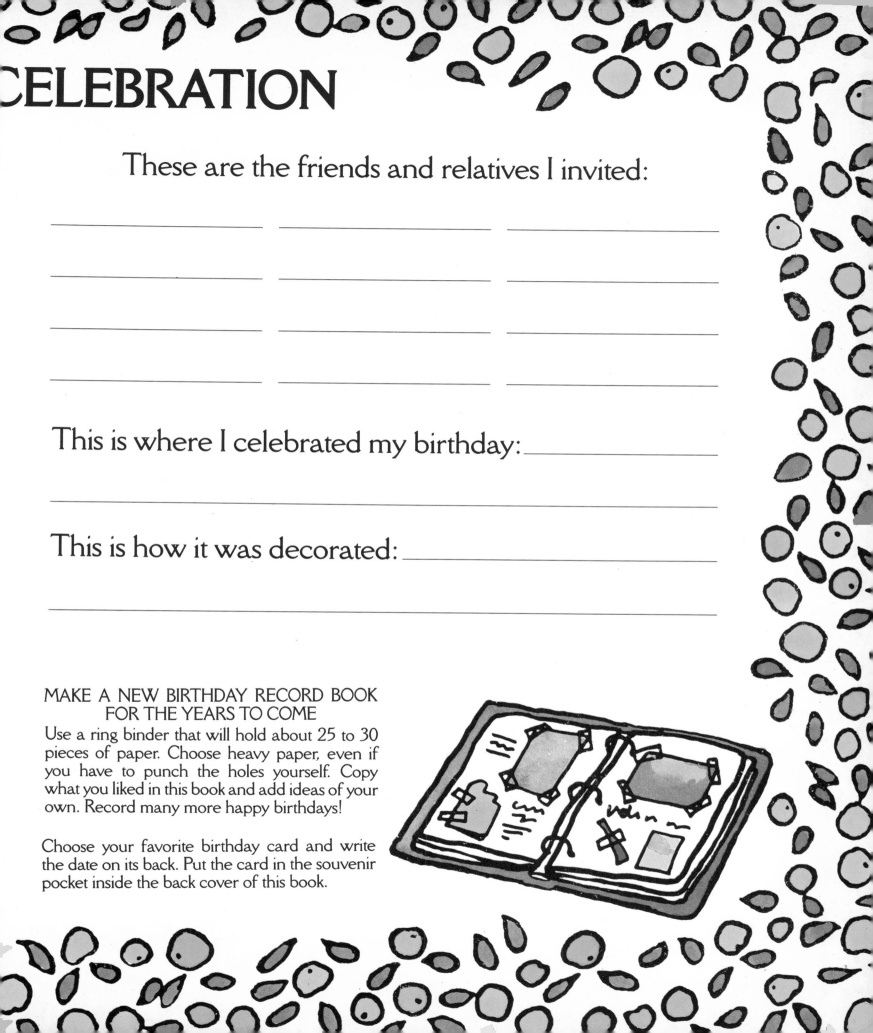

This is what we did at my birthday celebration:

_____

_____

_____

The best part was _____

_____

We ate
- ☐ beetles
- ☐ sandwiches
- ☐ cake and ice cream
- ☐ baseballs
- ☐ _____

something else

My birthday cake was
- ☐ chocolate
- ☐ vanilla
- ☐ orange
- ☐ mustard
- ☐ _____

something else

The frosting was
- ☐ chocolate
- ☐ vanilla
- ☐ strawberry
- ☐ glue
- ☐ _____

something else

Here is a picture of my birthday cake.

I blew out _____ candles.
how many?

This was my wish.
(Write it on a slip of paper or ask a grown-up to help you write it. Fold it and tape it in here.)

TOP SECRET

The wish I made last year ☐ came true

☐ didn't come true

☐ sort of came true

# Here is my favorite birthday picture.

Put extra pictures
in the pocket inside the
back cover of this book.

# These are the presents I received:

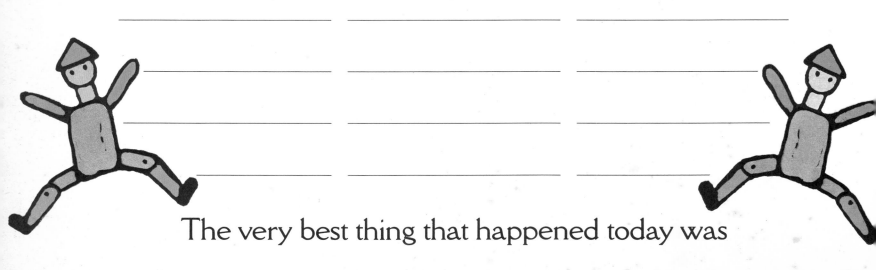

_____ _____ _____

_____ _____ _____

_____ _____ _____

_____ _____ _____

# The very best thing that happened today was

_____

# NEXT YEAR

Next year I will be _____ years old.
By my next birthday, I hope I will be able to

- ☐ climb Mount Everest
- ☐ reach the ceiling
- ☐ stand on my head
- ☐ ski in the Olympics
- ☐ bake a cake
- ☐ change a flat tire
- ☐ catch a butterfly
- ☐ talk to squirrels
- ☐ swim across a pool
- ☐ ride a bike
- ☐ run for President
- ☐ babysit
- ☐ jump higher
- ☐ charm a snake
- ☐ _____ something else

Each year on your birthday trace your hand here.